Look out for other books in this series:

& The Great Escape

Charlie
& The Big Snow

& The Rocket Boy

& The Cheese & Onion
Crisps

www.hilarymckay.co.uk

Charlie
& The Cat Flap

Hilary McKay

Illustrated by Sam Hearn

■SCHOLASTIC

First published in the UK in 2007
by Scholastic Children's Books
An imprint of Scholastic Ltd
Euston House, 24 Eversholt Street
London, NW1 1DB, UK
Registered office: Westfield Road, Southam, Warwickshire, CV47 0RA
SCHOLASTIC and associated logos are trademarks and or
registered trademarks of Scholastic Inc.

Text copyright © Hilary McKay, 2007
Illustrations © Sam Hearn, 2007
The right of Hilary McKay to be identified as the author of this work and of
Sam Hearn to be identified as the illustrator of this work has been asserted by them.
Cover illustration © Sam Hearn, 2007

10 digit ISBN 0 439 96879 8
13 digit ISBN 978 0439 96879 9

British Library Cataloguing-in-Publication Data
A CIP catalogue record for this book is available from the British Library

Typeset by Falcon
Printed in the UK by CPI Bookmarque, Croydon, CR0 4TD
Papers used by Scholastic Children's Books are made
from wood grown in sustainable forests.

7 9 10 8

www.scholastic.co.uk/zone

ONE

Four days before the Big Sleep

Charlie and Henry were
both seven years old, and
they were best friends.
They were best friends,
and they quarrelled all
the time. They argued at
school. They squabbled at birthday
parties. They nearly always had to be

separated on school trips. Their friends said, "Charlie and Henry have been like that for ever!" and took no notice; but their teachers called them The Terrible Two. "Double Trouble!" agreed Charlie and Henry's fathers.

Their mothers said,

"You boys ALWAYS end up quarrelling!"

One Monday morning, Charlie's big brother Max asked if he could stay with a friend for the night on Friday and his mother said he could. This would mean there would be an empty bed in Charlie's bedroom. That Monday afternoon, Charlie and Henry ran out of school to where their mothers were both standing moaning about them and Charlie asked, "On Friday night, can Henry come for a sleepover?"

Straight away Charlie and Henry's mothers said,

"No!"

"No," they said. "We haven't forgotten the last time!"

The last time Henry's father had had to get dressed at two o'clock in the morning and take Charlie home because Charlie said he could not bear listening to the way Henry breathed for one moment longer.

"He is copying my breathing!" Charlie had complained furiously. "Every time I breathe, he breathes! He has been doing it ever since you took away his Super Soaker Water Squirter! And what

3

has happened to my Itching Powder and my two dead flies? That's what I want to know!"

So Charlie had been taken home, and Henry's Super Soaker was banned for a week. But the Itching Powder and the two dead flies turned up safe and sound in Henry's bed, where Charlie had put them, and Charlie and Henry soon forgot all about their quarrel. They were astonished when their mothers reminded them. They looked at each other and they put on their Sad Little Boy faces and then they tried again.

Charlie said to his mother: "You let Max have sleepovers but you won't let me!"

"You like Max better than me!"

"He's your favourite!"

"It's not fair!"

And Henry said to his mother: "At least Charlie has Max! I have no brothers or sisters and I am fed up with living in a house just with grown-ups."

Their mothers made moaning sounds but Charlie and Henry did not stop.

They said: "We never quarrel!"

"Charlie likes it when I hit him."

"Henry likes it when I push him over."

"We only argue a bit."

"I don't argue," said Charlie.

"How can you say that?" asked Henry. "You argue all the time!"

"Just because I don't agree with every single word you say!" said Charlie.

"Argue argue argue," said Henry, sticking his thumbs in his ears and waving his fingers rudely at Charlie. "Moan moan moan!"

NER NER
NER NER
NER

"You think you are so clever!" said Charlie, grabbing at him. "You are not half as clever as you think you are!"

"You are not a quarter as clever as you think you are," replied Henry, dodging behind his mother.

"You are not a millionth!" shouted Charlie.

"You are not a quarter of a millionth!" said Henry.

Charlie was not very good at maths and he could not think of any amount smaller than a quarter of a millionth to say Henry was not as clever as, so he did not say anything. He stared up at the sky as if he did not care.

Henry came out from behind his mother and stuck out his tongue to show that he had won.

"Ha!" shouted Charlie, and jumped on Henry and tipped him on to the ground. It was always very easy for anyone to tip Henry over. He did not seem to be properly balanced.

Charlie sat down on top of Henry and Henry flung his arms about and bashed Charlie on the nose. It started to bleed at once. Charlie's nose always bled at the smallest bump. It did not seem to be very well made.

All this arguing and wrestling and nose bashing had taken less than two minutes.

And Charlie and Henry were still best friends at the end of it, but their mothers did not understand that. Henry's mother jerked Henry to his feet and said, "Now say you are sorry! Look what you've done to poor Charlie!"

Charlie's mother pushed a handful of tissues on to Charlie's nose and snapped,

"Sit still until it stops!"

"It is you who should

say sorry! Bumping down on poor Henry like that!"

Then both mothers exclaimed together,

"And you two are supposed to be friends!"

Charlie and Henry stopped asking if they could have a sleepover for the rest of that afternoon. But they agreed to start again the next morning (which was Tuesday). Patiently, maybe a hundred times, they asked the same question: "Why can't we have a sleepover?" Also Charlie said how his mother liked Max more than she liked him, and that it was not fair. And Henry said how tired he was of living with just grown-ups, and that it was not fair.

It was very hard work for Charlie and Henry, but in the end it worked. On Wednesday afternoon their mothers gave in and said, "Oh all right! Anything for peace and quiet! But this will be your Last Chance Ever!"

Two

Two days before the Big Sleep

Charlie and Henry planned the best
sleepover ever. They made an
agreement:

No Itching Powder, No Dead Flies
and No Super Soakers to be
squirted at the ceiling in order to make
surprise indoor rain.

"We'll look for ghosts," said Charlie.

"That's a good idea," said Henry. "And we'll have a midnight feast."

"Brilliant!" said Charlie.

It felt very strange saying "Good idea!" and "Brilliant!" to each other, but it was all part of Charlie and Henry's plan. They knew their sleepover would be cancelled if they began quarrelling, so for the next two days they were very polite. They did not fight at all, at least not where anyone could see them.

"It won't last," said Charlie's mother. She was in a very gloomy mood because the sleepover was happening at her house, but Henry's

mother (who was planning a trip to the cinema with her phone switched off) was much more cheerful. She said, "Perhaps Charlie and Henry are beginning to grow up. At last."

Then they both said, "Wouldn't it be lovely!"

It sometimes seemed to Charlie and Henry's mothers that Charlie and Henry were taking an awfully long time to grow up.

Charlie and Henry spent all their pocket money collecting food for the midnight feast. They bought salted peanuts, strawberry bootlaces, cheese triangles, Coca-Cola, chocolate M&Ms and curry-flavoured crisps. They hid all these things in the bottom of Henry's sleeping bag. Henry had carried his sleeping bag round to Charlie's house as soon as their mothers gave in and said the sleepover was allowed. Since then it had been kept in Charlie's bedroom in the bottom of the wardrobe that he shared with Max.

Charlie and Max had bunk beds. Max had the top bunk and Charlie had the bottom. Max would never let Charlie have a turn in the top bunk because sometimes Charlie had accidents at night.

"And what if it dripped through?" Max said. "And I was underneath! Horrible!"

Max did not like the idea of Charlie's sleepover. He said,

"You'd better not touch any of my stuff up here?"

"And you can tell Henry from me that he's to leave my skateboard and my bike alone this time! I wish he wasn't sleeping in my bed! I hope he doesn't do what you sometimes do!"

Charlie pretended not to hear.

"Well," said Max gloomily, "I suppose he's got a good thick sleeping bag!" He lifted Henry's sleeping bag out of the wardrobe, discovered the bulge in the bottom, and tipped it upside down.

"Those are our midnight feast supplies,"

said Charlie proudly, as salted peanuts, strawberry bootlaces, cheese triangles, chocolate M&Ms, curry-flavoured crisps and bottles of Coca-Cola tumbled on to the floor.

"Crikey!" said Max, even more gloomily. "If you eat that lot you'll both be sick for sure."

Charlie ignored that too.

"Still," continued Max, "maybe Henry won't be here long enough to eat it! Didn't Mum promise his mother she'd take him home the minute you started fighting?"

"Yes, well, we won't be fighting!" said Charlie. "And we won't be sick either! So ha ha! We're going to stay awake all night and look for. . . ghosts!"

"You two would be scared stiff if you saw a ghost!" Max laughed.

"We wouldn't!" Charlie said. "I wish we really could."

"You be careful what you wish for!" said Max, and in the middle of the night Charlie remembered those words.

THREE

The Big Sleep: eight o'clock till ten o'clock (at night)

Max left, and Henry arrived with a big square bag. Henry's mother had packed Henry's bag very carefully with everything he could possibly need. When she was not looking Henry had swiftly unpacked it again. So Henry had not brought pyjamas or slippers or washing things or anything like that. Instead he had brought his hamster in its cage. It took up the whole bag. Henry lifted the hamster cage up on to Max's bed and said, "I thought I could borrow stuff off you!"

Charlie didn't mind that at all. He got out a pair of his own pyjamas for Henry, and found a toothbrush he could use in the bathroom. After Charlie had sorted out Henry's pyjamas and toothbrush he suggested that they go for a treasure hunt through all Max's drawers and boxes in search of Interesting Secret Stuff. They treasure-hunted for a long time, but they did not find anything because Max had guessed this might happen and he had packed up all his Interesting Secret Stuff and taken it with him. Then they made Lego tanks and had a battle which got noisier and noisier until Charlie's mother came in and ordered, "Bed!"

Henry grumbled a bit about his pyjamas as they got ready for bed. He said they were pink but Charlie explained they were pale red. Henry

didn't say anything about the toothbrush (at the time).

When they were both ready, they went downstairs to say goodnight to Charlie's father and mother.

"Goodnight," said Charlie's father. "And remember, if there is any bother I will come and sleep on the floor and I warn you, I snore like a camel, don't I Charlie?"

"Yes," said Charlie proudly, and Henry said, "I bet you've never heard a camel snore!" So Charlie said, "How would you know what I've heard snore?"

Charlie's mother said hurriedly, "Night-night, boys, sweet dreams, don't talk too long! Are you wearing Charlie's pyjamas, Henry?"

"Yes," said Henry. "Mine got left at home. Do you mind?"

Charlie's mother said she didn't mind a bit. She said that as long as he and Charlie did not spend the night quarrelling about camels Henry could wear anything he liked. This was rather a silly thing to say, because as soon as Henry was back in the bedroom he put on Charlie's plastic suit of armour, and the shield and the sword belt and the sword. Then he clanked up the ladder to Max's top bunk where his sleeping bag was already unrolled, and lay down beside his hamster cage. "Pass me the bow and arrows, please, Charlie!" said Henry.

"No I won't!" said Charlie. "First you moan about my pyjamas, then you grab my suit of armour and now you want my bow and arrows!"

Charlie got out of his bunk and picked up the bow and arrows himself. Then he climbed on top of his chest of drawers and shot Henry as he lay in bed.

Henry said in a sad quiet voice, "I don't mind if you hurt me but please don't frighten my poor little hamster."

"You only said that to make me feel bad," said Charlie, fitting another arrow to his bowstring.

Henry did not reply. Instead, with great difficulty, he struggled out of the suit of armour and threw the pieces one by one at Charlie's head. Charlie fired his last arrow and made a rush for the top bunk, intending to pull Henry out and dump him on to the floor. From downstairs came a sudden voice.

"Are you boys behaving up there?"

"Yes!" shouted Charlie and Henry, letting go of each other.

"Nearly asleep?"

"Nearly," they called, diving under the covers and lying down flat.

"Shall I come up and see?"

"No,no,no!" yelled Charlie and Henry

with their eyes
tight shut.

For a long
time the room
was very quiet.
And it was very dark.

In the darkness Henry murmured,
"Charlie!"

Charlie nearly jumped out of his skin.
"What?" he asked.

"What if we heard
footsteps coming
louder and louder
up the stairs and
then suddenly the door
burst open with a huge bang
and cold air rushed into the room and a
great black shape towered over us and we
saw a green light all around and heard the

sound of screaming like in Harry Potter?"

"I don't know," said Charlie, not at all keen on thinking very hard about this idea.

"I only wondered," said Henry, "because it's gone very quiet downstairs and I think something horrible has happened to your mum and dad and it's going to happen to us next and I'm sure I saw the door move. Watch!"

Ten o'clock till midnight

Charlie watched the door and watched the door. He watched until his eyes hurt. All he could see was a grey shape, against a slightly lighter greyness, but it seemed to him that Henry was right, and that now and then it did move.

Henry moaned, "I hate your rotten sleepover!"

That made Charlie mad. "Big moaning baby!" he hissed.

"If you're so brave, why are you whispering?" demanded Henry. "Why don't you do something useful? Like shut the door."

"Because I don't want to," said Charlie.

"Oh yes!" said Henry. "I bet you're scareder than me!"

"Scaredy cat!"

"I'm not!" said Charlie, and to prove he wasn't, he bounced out of bed, closed the door properly, and began barricading it with all the biggest things in the room, his skateboard, his beanbag and, balanced on the top, his enormously heavy and rattly box of Lego. Then he snapped off the light and marched back to bed.

"Now you will be safe, poor little

Henry," said Charlie in a very kind voice.

Henry sighed and rolled over and got
his legs twisted up in his sleeping bag and
announced, "I need to go to the
bathroom!"

"You can't! I'd have to move all my
stuff!"

"Well, I do."

"I don't care. You'll have to wait till morning! Think about something else! When shall we have our midnight feast?"

"Midnight, of course," said Henry. "I don't know if I can wait till morning."

"Of course you can! Do you think it's nearly midnight?"

"No."

"Why not?"

"Because my light-up watch says half past ten."

"Oh," said Charlie crossly, because he had not got a light-up watch, and anyway was useless at telling the time. "Ages till midnight. We'd better go to sleep for a bit."

"I can't. I can't get to sleep."

"Count," advised Charlie. "Count yourself scoring goals. Max told me that. It works."

Henry
lay uncomfortably
beside his hamster cage and tried it.
He dressed himself up in a red and white
football strip, cut bright green grass into
perfectly patterned squares, filled the
largest arena in the world with cheering
fans, added a background of ten
magnificent red and white players not
quite as good as himself, an opposing team

in green and yellow, a terrified goalie
facing his charge (a goalie who looked
exactly like Charlie), and kicked relentless
penalties one after another with a ball that
left a trail of sparks in the air like a
comet's tail. Of course, with each goal the
crowd went crazy, and even the opposing
team couldn't help but cheer. In fact, as
Henry drifted off to sleep, everyone (and
there were thousands, not to mention all
the TV viewers) was having a wonderful
time except for the opposing team's goalie,
who would not admit he was frightened.

Suddenly there was the most enormous
sound in the world. And a bright light and
screaming. The screaming was Charlie.
And Henry, waking from a deep sleep, was
aware of a spreading warm dampness.

"Charlie, stop screaming!"
cried Charlie's mother. "It's
only me! I am so sorry!

I only thought I
would just peep
in! I had no
idea. . . Look at
this! Lego
everywhere! I'm
sorry I woke you
up, Henry! Go back
to sleep!"

The light went off again and Henry
became drowsily aware of Charlie,
grumbling to himself as he collected Lego
in the dark and rebuilt his fortifications.

"Crikey, that made an awful noise!"
murmured Henry as Charlie clambered
back into bed.

"I know," said Charlie. "I nearly wet the bed!"

"I think I did!"

"You did?"

"I think so."

"Want me to fetch Mum?"

"No. What'll I do?"

"Nothing," said the experienced Charlie. "It'll go away soon. It sort of disappears. I don't know why."

"OK," said Henry and sighed with relief, and then he asked, "How do you know?"

Charlie did not reply. He already felt he had

said too much. Instead he started to snore, and the more Henry said, "I know you can hear me! And I know you know what I mean!" the more he snored. So eventually Henry gave up. He went back to counting goals again, slightly damper than before, but on the whole much more comfortable. Charlie's snoring became part of the roar of the crowd. Henry fell asleep.

Midnight till two o'clock
(in the morning)

Henry was asleep, but Charlie was wide awake. He was sure he could hear something. Something alive, padding around the bedroom. Something sleek and black. A restless whisper that circled the bed. He did not know what time it was.

Charlie was too scared to move or make a sound and he had never felt so lonely.

Henry was no comfort at all. The person Charlie wanted most in the world was Max. Max was scared of nothing in the world. Not even ghosts.

Now Charlie was remembering what Max had said, when he, Charlie, had wished to see a ghost.

"Be careful what you wish for!"

The out-of-sight patch of blackness that was pacing the room seemed to come a little closer as Charlie remembered Max's words. Charlie's skin prickled and his heart thudded. He tried to breathe silently. He wondered if whatever-it-was knew where he was. And did it know that he was awake? And that his name was Charlie? And that he would do anything, promise anything, give anything – if only it would agree to get Henry instead of getting him.

It was right beside him now.

Charlie closed his eyes and waited to faint, and in the middle of his terror he thought how utterly unfair it was that of all the wishes he had ever made this one should be the only one to come true.

Then it jumped.

It jumped right past Charlie and up on to Henry's bunk and landed with a rattle on the hamster cage.

Charlie laughed aloud in relief. The thing that he had thought was a ghost was Suzy, the cat. She had finally located where the delicious smell of hamster was coming from.

"Yrrummmm!"said Suzy very happily.

"No Suzy!"

Charlie scrambled out of bed and on to the bunk-bed ladder and grabbed in the dark. Henry yelled and woke and sat up with a jerk that shook the cage and overbalanced Suzy. She fell on to Charlie, and Charlie fell on to floor and they landed together in a yowling, struggling heap.

Moments later the bedroom door was flung open and the Lego trap collapsed for the second time that night.

"What is it?" moaned Charlie's mother, her hair all on end and Charlie's father's dressing gown clutched around her, inside out. "Oh! Suzy! Suzy, you bad cat, whatever are you doing in here? Give her to me, Charlie, I'll put her outside. Are you all right, Henry?"

"Is that the cat that ate Charlie's hamster?" demanded Henry.

Charlie's mother made unhappy, don't-ask-me-horrible-questions-at-two-o'clock-in-the-morning noises, caught Suzy, and backed painfully over the Lego to the door.

"Is it?" asked Henry, extremely fiercely.

"I shall close your bedroom door and put her outside in the garden and put the catch on the cat flap so she can't get back in," said Charlie's mother, speaking as soothingly as she could between the pain of walking on Lego and an armful of scrabbling cat. "Go back to sleep, boys!"

She closed the door carefully behind her and Charlie and Henry sighed with relief because she had not noticed the hamster cage.

41

"That was so funny!" said Charlie, laughing.

"Funny!" exclaimed Henry. "Funny!" and he leant over the side of the bunk bed, grabbed a double handful of Charlie's hair and tugged. "That's for inviting my poor little hamster for a sleepover with a cannibal murdering cat!"

"I didn't invite your poor little hamster!" said Charlie, pulling away. "You brought it yourself!" And he laughed again and lay on his bed with his feet pushing

very hard at the underneath of Henry's mattress, so that it tipped alarmingly.

"I didn't know you'd still got that cat! Stop pushing my bed! S'not funny!"

"It is!"

Henry swiped as best he could below the bunk with his pillow.

"Missed!" said Charlie, choking with laughter, and pushed even harder.

Henry leaned dangerously far over the bunk rail and caught one of Charlie's legs. Charlie kicked and they both fell on to the floor. The bedroom door crashed open again and this time it was Charlie's father. His eyes were screwed nearly shut and he was wearing Charlie's mother's dressing gown, which was covered in peach-coloured frills.

"Ouch!" yelled Charlie's father, as he fell

over the skateboard and landed on the Lego.

"What the de. . . What the bl. . . What on earth. . ."

He switched on the light, caught sight of himself in the mirror, and switched it off again.

"I give up!" he groaned. "I'm much too old for performances like this. I'm going back to bed!"

Henry and Charlie went to bed too, very quietly in case he decided to change his mind and come back and sleep on the floor, as he had threatened to do.

Henry said, "Doesn't your dad know any proper swearwords?"

"Yes," said Charlie loyally. "He knows thousands! You wait till morning when he's properly awake!"

The house became quiet again. Charlie fell asleep, and Henry nearly fell asleep. Then he remembered something.

"Charlie!" he whispered.

"Mmmm?" groaned Charlie.

"We've got to eat that midnight feast!"

"We will," mumbled Charlie.

"When?"

"Soon," said Charlie, after a long, long

pause. "OK?"

There was no reply except a snore.

"Oh well," said Charlie, and very soon he was snoring too.

Two o'clock till four o'clock
(in the morning)

Henry's hamster was a very lazy animal.
Also he was used to living with Henry, who
was a bumpy, noisy sort of person to live
with. So the arrival of Suzy the cat on to
the top of his cage had not even caused
him to turn over in his sleep. But between
two and four o'clock in the morning he was
in the habit of getting up and running very

fast and excitedly in his little green exercise wheel. It made a screeching, rattling sound because it needed oiling. He also liked to chew the bars of his cage very hard. Henry's mother said it sounded just like the drill that men use to make holes in roads, but really it was not as bad as that.

However, it was still loud enough to wake up Charlie and Henry. They woke up as bright and alert as if they had just had ten hours' sleep instead of less than one. They discovered that they were both very hungry, and told each other what a good time it was to have a midnight feast.

"It's brilliant," said Henry. "Your mum and dad must be so exhausted by now that hardly anything could wake them up!"

Later on this turned out to be true.

Henry climbed down into Charlie's bunk and they got out the salted peanuts, the strawberry bootlaces, cheese triangles, Coca-Cola, chocolate M&Ms and curry-flavoured crisps, and they ate the lot. All except for one bit of cheese triangle, which they gave to the hamster.

"Max said

we'd be sick," remarked Charlie. "Do you feel sick?"

Henry sat for a while in silence to check the way he felt and then said, "Not really. Do you?"

"No," said Charlie, after checking carefully, and he added, "Max doesn't know everything!"

It was the first time in his life that Charlie had realized this. The idea made Charlie feel good. It made him feel fine and frisky.

The room was no longer dark. It was nearly four o'clock in the morning and because it was midsummer, dawn was not far away. Outside, a bird was beginning to sing. Charlie pulled back the curtain. The garden looked all green and silvery-grey and cool and empty.

"Let's go outside," said Charlie.

Before Henry's mother had left Henry at Charlie's house she had told him to be good. And so far, he thought, he had been. But now he had a feeling that sneaking out into the garden at four o'clock in the morning would not be being good at all.

Charlie said, in a very good little boy's voice, "It would be much nicer for my mother if we were sick outside instead of in here."

"I do feel a tiny bit sick!" said Henry at once.

"Well then," said Charlie solemnly, "we ought to go outside, Henry."

"Yes, Charlie," said Henry, just as solemnly. "I think we should."

So Charlie and Henry went barefoot and silently down the stairs, feeling that in all

ways they were doing
the right thing.

They were
very sorry to
find that the
kitchen door,
the door that led
into the garden,
was locked. The key
was nowhere in

sight. Charlie and Henry sat on the
doormat beside the cat flap and thought
and thought.

Afterwards, neither Charlie nor Henry
could remember which of them it was who
said, "Suzy is a big cat."

It was a big cat flap too, homemade by
Charlie's father, who was very clever at
making things. It had a catch on it which

could be moved so that it only opened one way. You could have it so that if Suzy went outside she could not get back in again, or so that if Suzy came into the house, she could not go back out again. Or you could leave the catch off altogether, so that Suzy could come and go as she pleased.

That night, Charlie's mother had fixed the catch so that after Suzy had been shooed out through the cat flap she could not come back in again.

"Suzy is a big cat," said whichever-of-them-it-was.

Then they had a short tussle on the doormat about who would go first and Henry won.

Henry stuck his head out of the cat flap, and then one arm, and then (wriggling sideways a bit) the other arm. After that, it

was easy for the rest of him to get through.
Charlie followed seconds later.

Four o'clock till six o'clock (in the morning)

It was wonderful in the garden. It was not dark at all any more. The grass was cool and wet with dew, and very slippery to bare feet.

Charlie and Henry played skids on the grass until their pyjamas were soaking wet with dew, and striped from top to bottom with green grass stains and mud. They

agreed that everyone who did not come out
and play skids on the lawn at five o'clock in
the morning was crazy. Charlie was perfectly
happy, and Henry was almost perfectly
happy except for one little thing. One tiny
little thing that had been at the back of his
mind, bothering him, since bedtime.

"Charlie," he said. "Where did you get
that toothbrush from that you lent me?"

Henry said this standing at the end of

the lawn. Charlie took a run and skidded towards him, sweeping his feet from under him so that he toppled like a skittle. Henry always did fall down very easily, but it still made him mad. So he bumped Charlie's head, which of course made Charlie's nose bleed. Then they were both mad, and Charlie would not answer Henry's question.

"I know it was not new," said Henry, when he had asked his question three or four times more, "because it wasn't in a packet and anyway it didn't taste new."

"How did it taste?" asked Charlie, interestedly.

"Old," said Henry.

"Oh," said Charlie, and he seemed to choke for a while, and then he said he was cold and he was going to go back to bed.

This time the cat flap was very, very hard to open. However, at last Charlie managed to force it far enough for him to get his head through. And one arm, but not the other.

All the time he was doing this Henry was demanding, "Where did that toothbrush come from?" and saying how old it had tasted. The more Henry thought about it, the older it seemed to him that the toothbrush had tasted.

At about half past five in the morning Charlie became completely stuck in the cat flap. The catch was bent from Charlie's forcing, so the cat flap was jammed half-open. Henry was no help at all. He just kept on and on about the toothbrush. So at last Charlie started shouting for help.

He could not shout very loudly, stuck on his stomach halfway through a very tight cat flap. After several minutes of calling, his parents still had not come down to rescue him. Henry had been right when he said that they must be so exhausted that hardly anything would wake them up.

Charlie was exhausted too. He said to Henry, "Ring the doorbell."

"What?" said Henry.

"Ring the doorbell," repeated Charlie, "and that will wake up Mum and Dad and they'll come downstairs and get me out."

Henry said he would only ring the doorbell if Charlie told him where the toothbrush had come from.

"You don't really want to know," said Charlie, which of course made Henry want to know more than ever. So at last, after a lot of arguing and promising and bargaining, Charlie agreed to tell him. And Henry agreed to ring the doorbell straight after.

Then they fell into complete silence.

"Go on then," said Henry at last.

"It was my grandma's," said Charlie.

"WHAT!!!!" yelled Henry, and he ran around the garden with his tongue hanging out, shaking his head and roaring, and then he licked handfuls of grass, and

RRAAARGH!

after that he came back and demanded
furiously, "Which grandma?"

"Ring the doorbell!" begged Charlie.

"Which grandma?" shouted Henry. "The
big hairy one or the one you only let come
at Christmas?"

"The one we only let come at Christmas,"
said Charlie. "Now ring the doorbell!"

Then at last Henry did ring the
doorbell. But before he did it he gave
Charlie the most enormous stinging wallop
on the part of him that was still sticking
out of the cat flap.

EIGHT

Six o'clock in the morning onwards

Charlie's father and mother were very surprised and furious when they saw where Charlie was. Charlie's father said he had a good mind to leave him there, and just use the front door from now on.

"Good idea," said Charlie's mother, and started to go back to bed, but then she said, "but I can't be going right round by the front door every time I want to hang the washing out."

So they decided to rescue Charlie after all. His father unscrewed the bent catch and pulled him through the cat flap. They would not let Henry follow, even though he tried to. They let him in the ordinary way through the door.

Charlie's father and mother were not a bit sorry for Charlie, even though he was very sore, and covered in mud and blood and grass stains. They were not very polite to Henry either. Both boys were sent upstairs for a bath and a shower.

"Not a bath or a shower, a bath and a shower," said Charlie's mother.

"This has been the second worst night of my life!"

She sounded so fierce that they did not

even dare ask which had been the first
worst. They did not dare to complain
either. They crawled upstairs in silence,
but when they were in the bathroom
Henry caught sight of Charlie's grandma's
toothbrush. It made him groan and moan
and drink a lot of bathroom water out of
the tooth mug.

"Sorry," said Charlie to Henry.

Then they had a look at the bright red

hand print that was glowing on Charlie's bottom. Henry had done that, and he had meant it to hurt, and he could see that it did.

"Sorry," he said to Charlie.

By the time they came out of the bathroom, very clean and scrubbed looking, Charlie's father had gone to work. And Charlie's mother was quite calm, even though she had now seen the state of Charlie's bedroom, which was more or less covered in Lego and hamster cage sawdust and the remains of the midnight feast.

"Well at least you seem to have stopped quarrelling!" she said.

This surprised Charlie and Henry, who were best friends and thought they hardly ever quarrelled.

Another surprising thing happened

when Henry's mother came to collect
Henry.

Henry's mother asked (in a very
worried voice), "Well, how did it go?"

"I suppose," said Charlie's mother,
carefully not looking at Charlie and Henry,
"I suppose they could have been much
worse!"

Charlie and Henry's eyes met over the
breakfast table, and their jaws dropped
open in surprise. Looking back on the
night, they themselves really could not see
how they could have been much worse.

So then Henry's mother said, "How
good! Then perhaps Charlie could come for
a sleepover at our house next Saturday!"

Charlie and Henry now waited for
Charlie's mother to tell the truth. This did
not happen.

"Yes," said Charlie's mother, very eagerly. "Yes he could! That would be lovely!"

"He could bring his school things and stay for the whole weekend if you like!" suggested Henry's mother.

Charlie and Henry shook their heads in disbelief, and they thought that even if they lived to be as old as their mothers, they would never understand the ways of grown-ups.

"That would be wonderful!" said Charlie's astonishing mother, and she shooed the boys outside and began to make coffee for herself and Henry's mother. Henry's mother watched in astonishment as she poured milk into the coffee jar and then tried to push the kettle in the fridge.

"Gosh, sorry!" said Charlie's mum. "Bit sleepy!"

Henry's mother thought of the coming Saturday night and felt suddenly frightened.

Outside in the garden things were much more cheerful. Charlie had just tipped Henry over. Henry was making grabs for Charlie's nose. It looked like they were fighting, but of course they were not.

They were perfectly happy.

They were best friends.

Meet Charlie – he's trouble!

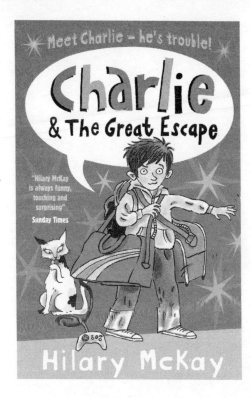

Charlie's fed up with his mean family always picking on him – so he's decided to run away. That'll show them! Now they'll be sorry!

But running away means being boringly, IMPOSSIBLY quiet…

Meet Charlie – he's trouble!

"The snow's all getting wasted! What'll we do? It will never last till after school!"

Charlie's been waiting for snow his whole life, but now it's come, everyone's trying to spoil it! Luckily, Charlie has a very clever plan to keep it safe…